Snowsong Whistling

Snowsong Whistling

by **KAREN E. LOTZ**

illustrated by **ELISA KLEVEN**

DUTTON CHILDREN'S BOOKS

· *New York* ·

Text copyright © 1993 by Karen E. Lotz
Illustrations copyright © 1993 by Elisa Kleven
All rights reserved.
CIP Data is available.
Published in the United States 1993 by Dutton Children's Books,
a division of Penguin Books USA Inc.
375 Hudson Street, New York, New York 10014
Designed by Sara Reynolds
Printed in Hong Kong
First Edition
1 3 5 7 9 10 8 6 4 2
ISBN 0-525-45145-5

*The art in this book is mixed-media collage, using watercolors,
gouache, pastels, ink, cut paper, cloth, and lace.*

to all the children of autumn and winter

by birth or by spirit

(Donna and Elisa, in particular)

and also, especially, to bluegills

K.E.L.

to Larry and Lila

E.K.

There's a crisp in the air

From I-don't-know-where

But it might be

A snowsong whistling.

It lifts and it purls

While it flits and curls

And it could be

A snowsong whistling.

Pumpkins plumping

Bluegills jumping

Apples thumping

Sweet cider pumping

Chestnuts bowling

Threshers rolling

School bells tolling

Groundhog holing

Hot pies baking

Chimney smoke snaking

Scarecrow faking

Cornstalks aching

A feast or a dance

Is a romp of a chance

To celebrate

A snowsong whistling.

You waltz and you jig

And you zag and zig

To notes swirling from

The snowsong whistling.

Red squirrels packing

Hound dog tracking

Leaf fires crackling

Farmers stacking

Chill wind teasing

Kitten half-sneezing

Radiator wheezing

Pond water freezing

Yellow yams steaming

Cooky dough creaming

Small fry dreaming

Skate blades gleaming

As the steady hoofbeats drum

Gliding runners start to hum—

Jingling sleigh bells join

The snowsong whistling.

Soon we'll all know why

Ringing low beneath the sky

Echoes chorus from

The snowsong whistling.

Ankles wobbling

Cold ears throbbing

Turkeys gobbling

Neighbors hobnobbing

Mistletoe blooming

Teakettle fuming

Father cat grooming

Storm clouds looming

Brindled dog bristling

Cardinals trysting

Frost feathers glistening

Snowsong whistling

WINTER'S COME!

Snowsong's sung.